THE MUCH TOO LOVED QUILT

by Rachel Waterstone
Illustrated by Marnie Webster

First Story Press

To my husband and children with love.
--M.W.

To my family and all my friends.
--R.W.

First Edition

First Story Press
Clarksville, Tennessee
1-888-754-0208

Library of Congress Cataloging-in-Publication Data
Waterstone, Rachel.
The much too loved quilt / by Rachel Waterstone; illustrated by Marnie Webster.
p. cm.
Summary: The students in Room 213 learn an important lesson as the special quilt the class had made is changed when each child takes it home.
ISBN 1-890326-15-1
[1. Quilts Fiction. 2. Schools Fiction.]
I. Webster, Marnie, ill. II. Title.
PZ7.W264375Mu 1999
[E]--dc21 99-25115
CIP

Printed in China

The kids in Room 213 could be heard clear down the hall.

"Draw my name, Miss Lane!" "No mine!" "I wanna be first!"

Miss Lane stood ready to draw a name for the first student to take the classroom quilt home. Each had designed and made a quilt square. The class had worked to sew the squares into a quilt. Now each student would have a turn to take the finished quilt home for a weekend.

Noisy Room 213 quieted down.

"The first to take 'The Much Loved Quilt' home will be Amanda," Miss Lane announced.

"Oh darn!" said the kids as they all began talking once again.

Amanda took her place by the folded quilt. "I brought a special shopping bag for us to carry our perfect quilt home in," she told everyone. "We can take good care of the quilt so it won't get dirty."

The Much Loved Quilt
707
Amanda
SWIM TEAM
Sandy
Soccer
1 2 3
4 5 6
7 8 9

That night, Amanda folded the quilt neatly at the foot of her bed. She thought of Room 213. Those students were the messiest. The loudest. The worst behaved. Except for her, of course. She knew the kids from Room 213 tried hard to be good, but sometimes they just could not. Miss Lane would say, "Room 213 isn't perfect, but you don't have to be perfect to be loved."

"Be careful and don't get the quilt dirty," Amanda told Tommy when it was his turn.

Tommy knew he had to be very careful with the quilt, but he thought it would be okay for his baby sister to play on the quilt with its colorful squares.

"This quilt took a lot of hard work," Tommy said as he did his math homework. "Isn't it pretty with all of its squares?"

When the baby made a funny gurgle, Tommy turned around. The baby then made a funny face.

"Oh no!"

The next morning, Tommy looked sadly at the quilt.

"Don't worry," his mother said. "Most of the stain came out. There's just a little mark where Amanda embroidered her name. I'm sure she won't even notice."

"This is a catastrophe!" Amanda shrieked when she saw the quilt the next day at school. "How could this have happened? Miss Lane, look what happened to our quilt! Look at my patch!"

When it was her turn, Kayla couldn't wait to show her school bus friends the quilt. On the bus, she unfolded it carefully so it wouldn't get dirty.

"Hey, let me look!" roared the bus bully, leaping from his seat at the back of the bus where he always sat.

RIIIIIP! Kayla stepped on a corner of the quilt when she tried to keep it from him.

"Your ol' quilt isn't so perfect now," the bus bully snickered.

EXIT

Amanda scrunched her face when she saw how Kayla had tried to sew the tear. She tried hard to think about how Miss Lane would say, "A little spot here. A little tear there. We love our quilt anyway."

When Tyler took the quilt home, Amanda reminded him not to get the quilt dirty. "It won't get dirty," he told her for the zillionth time.

At home, one of his friends shouted an idea, "Get in the middle and we'll throw you up in the air!"

"The quilt won't get dirty, will it?" Tyler asked.

"Naaah," everyone said.

"Will you sign my cast?" Tyler asked on Monday when he gave the quilt to Miss Lane. The kids in Room 213 gathered around.

"I fell on Andrew and bumped his front tooth," Tyler said."The quilt got a little blood stain on it . . . It didn't get dirty though."

Amanda's mouth dropped.

Leaves
Trees
AMANDA

When Mim took the quilt home, she told Amanda she wouldn't get the quilt dirty because she was only going to show it to friends at an outdoor wedding shower her mother was having.

"I can tell you about each special patch," Mim said to the girls.

Mim's patch was made from her grandmother's apron. One patch was made from a soccer jersey. Another was from a favorite pumpkin Halloween costume. One was a rainbow of paint and fabric on a square.

Suddenly sprays of water squirted everywhere. The lawn sprinklers! The girls screamed. Mother and her friends screamed.

Quickly Mim's mother turned off the sprinklers. Mim picked up the soggy quilt.

"We will just put it into the dryer," her mother said.

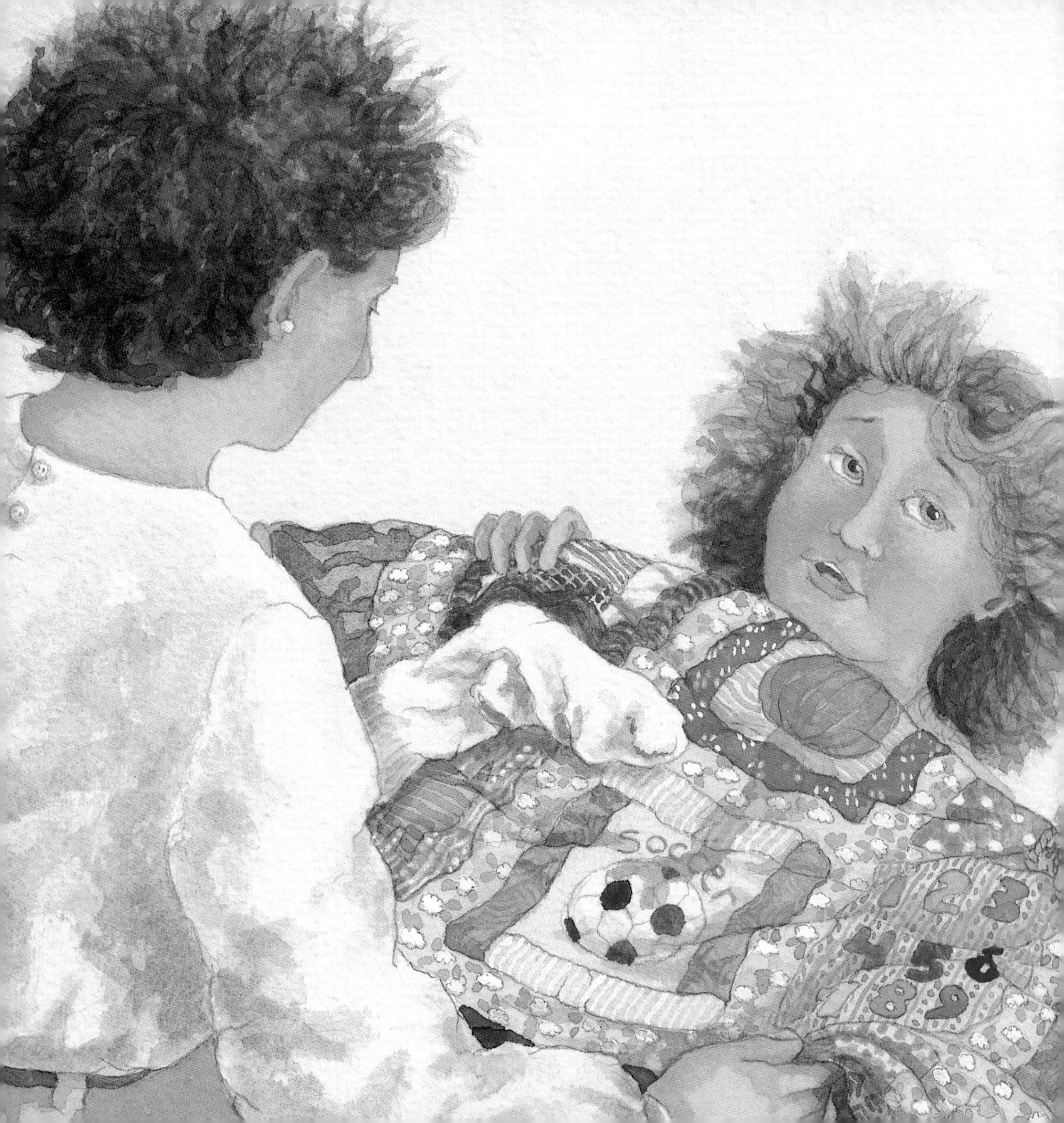

The next morning, Mim returned the quilt to class. Snapping with static electricity, it had a sock clinging to it. Some of the orange from the Halloween costume had faded onto the white of the soccer patch. The quilt had even shrunk a little in places.

"Here's the quilt. It's nice and clean," Mim said as she handed it to Miss Lane. "But, it did stay in the dryer a little too long."

Amanda blinked back tears.

Finally the day arrived for the quilt to be hung in the classroom. Once again, the kids from Room 213 could be heard clear down the hall. They talked. They made messes. They got in each other's way.

"Let me help!" "I'll help too!" "I want to hold it!"

Amanda unhappily looked at the changes in the quilt as she helped Miss Lane.

To get a better look, Amanda pulled on the quilt. A red ink line from Miss Lane's marker streaked across a patch. But, no one shrieked. No one's face scrunched. No one's mouth dropped. No tears appeared.

"That's okay, Amanda," everyone agreed. "Quilts don't have to be perfect. And, neither do people."

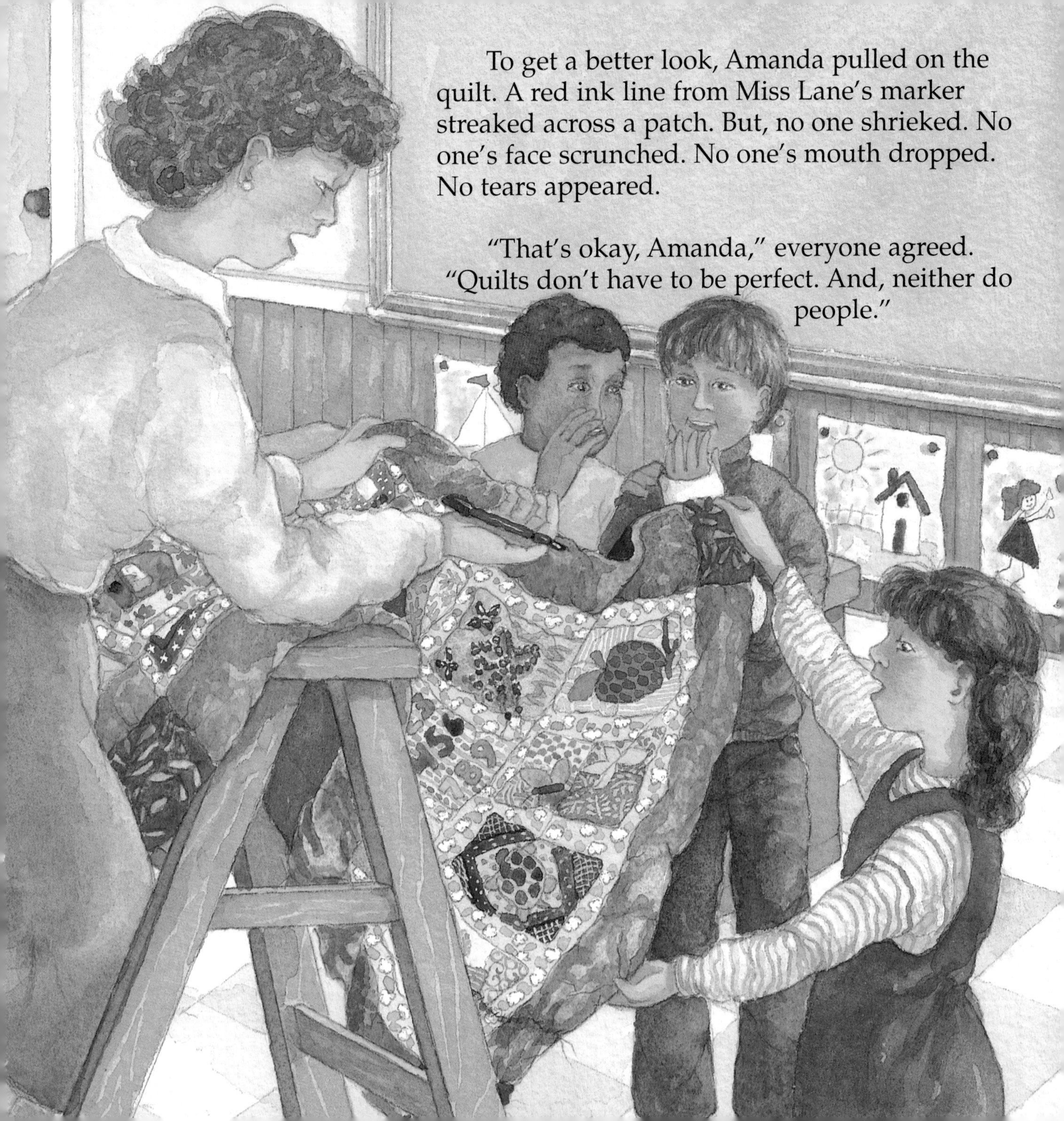

Then the kids from Room 213 all talked at once as they finished hanging their not-so-perfect but much loved quilt.